For Noah and Yannik, loving brothers.
And for Paula Wiseman, editor of superior magnitude.
—T. J.

For my sister, Martha, who's sweet, not smelly.
—E. D.

SIMON & SCHUSTER BOOKS FOR YOUNG READERS
An imprint of Simon & Schuster Children's Publishing Division
1230 Avenue of the Americas, New York, New York 10020
Text copyright © 2019 by Johnston Family Trust • Illustrations copyright © 2019 by Emily Dove
SIMON & SCHUSTER BOOKS FOR YOUNG READERS is a trademark of Simon & Schuster, Inc.
For information about special discounts for bulk purchases, please contact Simon & Schuster Special
Sales at 1-866-506-1949 or business@simonandschuster.com.
The Simon & Schuster Speakers Bureau can bring authors to your live event.
For more information or to book an event, contact the Simon & Schuster Speakers
Bureau at 1-866-248-3049 or visit our website at www.simonspeakers.com.
Book design by Chloë Foglia • The text for this book was set in Usherwood.
The illustrations for this book were rendered digitally and with watercolor.
Manufactured in China
1118 SCP • First Edition
2 4 6 8 10 9 7 5 3 1
Library of Congress Cataloging-in-Publication Data
Names: Johnston, Tony, 1942– author. | Dove, Emily, 1985– illustrator.
Title: Spencer and Vincent, the Jellyfish brothers / Tony Johnston ; illustrated by Emily Dove.
Description: First edition. | New York : Simon & Schuster Books for Young Readers, [2019] | "A Paula Wiseman Book." |
Summary: When jellyfish brothers Spencer and Vincent are separated during a big storm,
it will take the help of many friends and all of their brotherly love to reunite them.
Identifiers: LCCN 2018016738| ISBN 9781534412088 (hardcover) | ISBN 9781534412095 (eBook)
Subjects: | CYAC: Brothers—Fiction. | Jellyfishes—Fiction. | Love—Fiction. |
Marine animals—Fiction. | Humorous stories.
Classification: LCC PZ7.J6478 Spe 2019 | DDC [E]—dc23
LC record available at https://lccn.loc.gov/2018016738

SPENCER
and
VINCENT
THE JELLYFISH BROTHERS

Story by Tony Johnston   *Pictures by* Emily Dove

A Paula Wiseman Book
Simon & Schuster Books for Young Readers
New York   London   Toronto   Sydney   New Delhi

Spencer and Vincent were brothers.

Spencer was a jellyfish.

Vincent was also.

They lived together in the sea, their wet and shining home. Their dear mother and father were gone. So they only had each other.

Spencer and Vincent invented a little song,
which went like this:

They often regaled each other with this ditty as they
blobbed along over the foaming ocean waves.
Spencer and Vincent loved each other to the very
core of their jelly, as only brothers can.

One morning (at eight to be precise) a storm brewed up from a far place (Patagonia perhaps). Clouds gloomed over the wet and shining sea. Waves bloomed up. Waves blammed down. And oh, golly day—one wave of superior magnitude (that is, really hugely ENORMOUS) swept Vincent away!

"Help, Spencer! Save me!" screeched Vincent in a frightened voice as the wave of superior magnitude swashed him into the distant distance.

"I'm coming!" yelled Spencer.

He tried bravely to speed his way to Vincent.
But he was racing slowly. Pathetically slowly.

How fast can jellyfish speed? Spencer was in essence a floater. A bobber of seas. A blob. A lump. In normal times, he could pulse himself along to some degree. But not in these high seas.

I know somebody of superior magnitude who can help, Spencer thought. So he blobbed up to that somebody.

"Horace," said Spencer in a most sympathetic way, "please, oh, please, help me find my brother, swept away by a wave of superior magnitude."

Horace, his friend whale, said, "Okay. Which way did he go?"

"That way." Spencer pointed his many tentacles excitedly.

Horace lunged himself and plunged himself over the wild and salty sea.

Ahead of him he nudged Spencer,

ever on the lookout for Vincent, his brother.

Along the way Spencer asked a mermaid he knew, "Have you seen my brother?"

"Your brother who's sweet, not smelly?"

"Yes, that brother."

"He was swashed that way by a wave of superior magnitude," said the mermaid singingly. All scaly and shimmery, she pointed toward a distant island.

"Thanks," Spencer said. And he pulsed on, nudged by good Horace, the whale of superior magnitude.

"Have you seen my brother?" cried Spencer in desperation to anybody he came upon.

A seahorse rose up from a forest of kelp.

"Have you seen my brother?" asked Spencer.

"Your brother who's sweet, not smelly?"

"Yep, that brother."

"Yes, I saw him," the seahorse neighed.

Unfurling his tail, he showed the way.

Spencer blobbed on frantically.

"Have you seen my brother?" Spencer kept calling through the limpid ocean water.

A sea star called from an outcropping of rock, "Your brother who's sweet, not smelly?"

"Yes, that brother."

"Yeah, I saw him." Then the sea star clammed up.

"Where?" Spencer shouted, as loud as a jellyfish possibly can.

"There." The sea star waved an arm toward a beach.

Sure enough, off in the distance blobbed Vincent.
He looked woozy, dizzy, dazed, and stunned from the storm.
But—how grand!—he was afloat on the water, not stranded on the sand.

Spencer was overjoyed to the depth of his jelly.
But he didn't go near, for fear of being beached.
By now, all the ocean creatures Spencer had met—and gobs of others—were
eager to help him save Vincent, his brother. They crowded closer and closer.

Suddenly, a passing pelican dove down.

"Hold fast! I'll scoop him up!" he declared.

He swooped low, beak open to slurp Vincent.

"Please don't!" Spencer shouted, concerned that the
pelican might swallow Vincent (of course, by accident).

Everybody understood the tug of brotherly love—even the
plummeting pelican. In mid-dive he swerved off to somewhere else.
Haste was of the essence.

"Stand back, friends! I'm rushing in!" yelled Spencer, despite his fear
of being washed up on the sand.

He rushed as fast as a jellyfish can.

Then he thought of a better plan.
He remembered their song.

He gathered all his jellyfish self together.

He blasted with all his jellyfish heart:

My brother, my brother,
he's sweet, not smelly.
I love him from down in my jelly belly.

That sound perked Vincent up.
The sound of his brother's voice.
Vincent blinked his eyes. "Brother,"
he whispered, all groggy and limp,
"I don't think I can make it."

"YES, YOU CAN!" called Spencer inspirationally.

As one, the gathered sea folk chorused,

"YES, YOU CAN!"

From Spencer's words, Vincent took heart. With his last spark of verve, he slurped himself feebly toward Spencer.

Then Horace smacked a fluke of superior magnitude and sent a foaming wave.

The wave swashed Vincent up, floating him to Spencer.

In a tenderness of tentacles the brothers clasped each other,
an embrace of superior magnitude. Then, nudged by the good
whale Horace, they blobbed upon the foaming ocean waves,
all the wet way home.

Author's Note

Maybe you have seen a jellyfish somewhere and wanted to know more about it. Jellyfish are not fish at all. They are gelatinous zooplankton, simple, boneless beings that have been on earth for millons and millions of years.

"Plankton" means drifter, and drift is what jellyfish do. Some float upon the surface. Some wander through deeper waters. Others become bottom dwellers.

Jellyfish live in salt water and fresh and have nicknames like Flying Saucer, Purple People Eater, and Santa's Hat. They are mostly slow, often pulsing themselves along. The jellyfish that people know best have poisonous tentacles that trail behind them for protection and to stun small fish and other things they eat. The deadly box jellyfish of Australia and Indonesia is the most poisonous animal in the world.

There are many different types of jellyfish. More are being discovered every day. Jellies come in many sizes. The largest can grow to about ten feet wide, with stinging tentacles ribboning out almost one hundred feet. They can be colorful, but most are transparent—that is, you can see through them. Being invisible may be a defense against creatures wanting to eat them. It might also help them sneak up on their own dinners. Perhaps to surprise and hold off foes, some jellyfish glow.

Jellyfish have many enemies, like crabs, sharks, sea turtles, seabirds, and other jellyfish—even people. But in this story, most of the ocean community is friendly, pulling together to rescue a brother. Whatever they may do, Spencer and Vincent are fictional characters floating upon the whimsical ocean of imagination.

—T. J.